This Book
Presented to

Evergreen
Academy
1993

By
Denise True

B311

Denise True donated this book
to our library. Denise knows the
author and Denise is the girl with
the long braid on page 10.
                    July 1, 1993

A Choices for the Earth Book

Joe's Earthday Birthday

by Karen Scovel with Ted Hunter

illustrated by Jean Whitney

To all the great kids at Evergreen Academy. You're terrific!! Best regards, Karen Scovel 7/1/93

and Denise Kate bh raule

EARTH FRIENDLY PRESS

An Imprint of Parenting Press, Inc.

Seattle, WA

We would like to thank ten-year-old
Anne Odell for suggesting the title,
Joe's Earthday Birthday.

Book and cover design by:
Patrick Howe/ Design Source

ISBN 0-943990-84-X Paper
ISBN 0-943990-85-8 Library binding
LC 92-85492

An Earth Friendly Press Book
Published by Parenting Press, Inc.
P.O. Box 75267
Seattle, WA 98125

Published in association with:
Pacific Energy Institute
600 1st Ave, #400
Seattle, WA 98104

Pacific Energy Institute's mission is to
provide innovative solutions to enhance
the efficient use of resources and thereby
foster a sustainable future. A nationally
recognized nonprofit organization, PEI
educates businesses, schools, and families
in energy conservation and waste reduction.

"**DON'T** order any weird stuff on the pizza," said Justin.

"I won't. Since it's my party, I can order whatever I want," answered Joe. He and his best friend Justin were in the tree house, planning Joe's birthday party.

"Don't forget," added Justin, "David's birthday party is before yours. I think it's tomorrow."

David was one of their friends. He had the best parties in the neighborhood. His parents always put up the best decorations and gave the most party favors. Sometimes they got tired of the way David bragged about his parties, but they were always glad when they were invited.

David had promised that this year's party would be "out of this world." He was right. His apartment was decked out with streamers that hung from the ceilings and light fixtures. Helium balloons and styrofoam balls were painted to look like planets and stars. The gift table was covered with a blue paper tablecloth with a picture of a spaceship. Another table had the same kind of tablecloth with matching paper plates, cups, napkins, and plastic forks and spoons. The coolest decoration was the giant cardboard spaceship, just like the one on the tablecloth and dishes.

But something was missing. Joe looked worriedly around the room for the party favors. Ah, there they were! Ten plastic bags full of treasures.

After the party, Joe and Justin played in the left-over wrappings with David.

"Mission Control, Mission Control. We've hit a meteor shower!" Justin bellowed into his hand while making crackling sounds to imitate a radio.

He hurled a big ball of wrapping paper across the room. The floor had disappeared under a sea of discarded paper and boxes from the presents. David and Joe pretended they were giant crater worms, slithering under the paper to stalk Justin.

"Joe, your mom is here," David's mom called. "David, after you tell your friends good-bye, you can help clean up this mess."

"But, Mom!" David complained, "It's my birthday."

"Maybe Joe and Justin can help you carry out the trash as they leave."

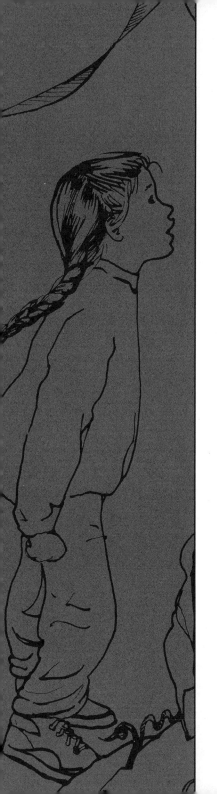

THE boys smashed and crushed the bags of paper into the garbage bin as best they could. David's little sister, Denise, followed them.

She made a face at David, "My teacher says we should recycle our paper so we don't have to cut down more trees or use up our land for garbage dumps."

David hated it when his sister told him what to do – especially in front of his friends.

"Denise, the paper from my party won't make any difference. Besides, Mom asked us to do this."

JOE stared at the overflowing garbage bin as they drove off. The lid wouldn't fit tightly because of all the paper. He saw David's mom bringing out another load of garbage and setting it on the ground next to the bin.

"It's pretty quiet back there," said Joe's mom. "Did you guys have fun?"

"Yeah, it was okay," Joe answered. Justin rummaged through the wrappers left in his party bag to make certain he hadn't missed any more pieces of candy. He pulled out his party favor—a plastic toy telescope, already broken.

"JUSTIN, did you hear what Denise said about the garbage?" Joe asked.

"You mean about recycling?"

"Yeah. David said the paper from his party didn't matter. He always thinks he knows everything, but he doesn't. We learned about recycling in school. Mr. Martin said we *all* have to recycle, all the time, or the earth won't get better. If we cut down all the trees, we won't even have air to breathe."

"My dad says we don't even know what we'll do when we run out of room to dump garbage," Justin added. "That's soooo gross! What if we had to keep garbage in the house all year long?"

Joe and Justin laughed—it was such a disgusting thought!

"I'VE got an idea!" Joe said suddenly. "Mom," he called up to the front seat, "I don't want to have my birthday party at that pizza place anymore. Can we do my party at home so we can show David that his way isn't the only way to have fun? We could build an awesome robot and fix up the treehouse in the back yard without using up so much paper, and..." Joe bounced excitedly in his seat.

"I know, you can tell everyone who comes they can't bring anything that has to go in the garbage!" Justin added.

"Well, there are times when we need things that just have to go in the garbage," said Joe's mom, "but I think it's great that you know there is more to waste reduction than just recycling. Your party could show your friends how to reduce and re-use, too. How can I help?" She was proud of the boys. If only more people would think about ways to reduce the garbage they make, she thought.

16

THE next few days Joe and his family got ready for the party. The invitations asked kids to bring a bag of recyclables to be used for a secret project. They decided the menu would be pizza, cake, and ice cream.

Even though it would be his birthday, Joe agreed to help wash dishes and do laundry after the party, so they wouldn't have to use paper dishes or napkins.

"Do you think he might be coming down with something?" Joe's stepdad teased, but he was proud of Joe, too.

Even Joe's little sister, Cassie, helped with the decorations by using ribbons from their grandma's fabric bag and by picking flowers.

They went shopping the night before the party after Joe's mom's meeting. They bought the food and two glass bottles full of chocolate milk—Joe's favorite drink. They didn't want juice boxes because glass is easier to recycle. Most importantly, they bought the party favors: ceramic mugs for every guest and the birthday kid, of course. This way everyone could drink their chocolate milk in a special mug and take it home to keep and reuse for a long time.

WHEN the doorbell rang the next day, Joe ran to open the door. It was his older cousin Dan, who came to help with the secret project. Next to him stood David, the know-it-all.

"I never thought I'd be bringing garbage to a birthday party. What a dumb idea," David complained.

Suddenly, Joe didn't feel so excited. Then he saw Justin come up the sidewalk. Under one arm he carried a present wrapped in the Sunday comics and tied up with ropes of licorice! He carried a bag of recyclables in his other hand. Joe felt happy again.

The backyard looked great. The recycling bins for paper, glass, plastic, and cans were cleaned up, decorated, and set below the treehouse. The bin was an easy target for any paper the kids wanted to throw out of the treehouse.

JOE and his friends never dreamed a party could be so much fun. They made phones out of cans and string, connecting the treehouse to an outpost in the yard, so they could talk to each other. A rousing game of "kick the can" worked up their appetites. Even David had fun building a bird feeder out of plastic bottles.

But the secret project—the robot—was the real hit of the party. Each friend added some recyclable thing they'd brought. Dan hooked up some blinking lights inside it, and installed a hidden voice synthesizer, which picked up the sounds of the kids around it. Everyone wanted their picture taken with "Recycle Man."

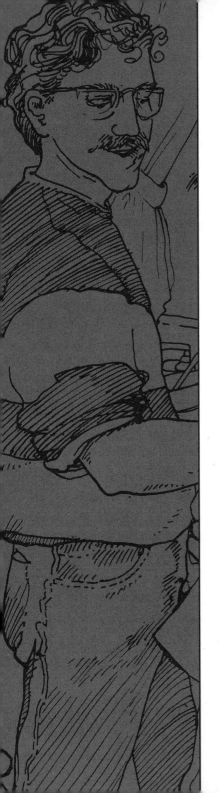

AFTERWARDS, Joe and his stepdad did the dishes. "I've never seen so many kids in the treehouse at once," his stepdad remarked.

"Everyone wanted to throw paper into the recycling bin from up there. Next to the presents and the robot, that was my favorite part of the party," Joe said, tired but happy.

"Whew! There are a lot of dishes. Are you still glad you made your party so earth-friendly?" asked his stepdad.

Just as Joe was about to answer "yes," Dan walked into the kitchen with paper and pencil in hand.

"Hey, Joe," he said, "I just figured out that if everyone in your school had a party like David's this year, the garbage would fill the cafeteria clear to the ceiling! But if they had an earth-friendly party, like yours, all the garbage would fit in two garbage cans. That's pretty cool."

J OE made a birthday wish. At first he wished the dishes were done, but then he decided to change it. He thought, I wish we *all* would think about the earth before planning parties.

The End

The Dirty Rotten Low-Down Stinking Truth About Garbage

(Fun Facts About Waste and Recycling)

Did you know that...

...in the United States, we each throw out an average of four pounds of garbage a day, which adds up to 160 million tons of garbage each year? That's enough to bury 27,000 playing fields in a layer of garbage 10 feet high!

...paper is the single largest cause of waste and one of the simplest materials to recycle? Paper products made from recycled paper use as much as 70% less energy to produce than products made from wood pulp.

...the United States is the largest garbage producer in the world? For every garbage can filled in Japan, the U.S. fills up four.

...all paper products should be recycled? For every ton of paper that we put into the recycle bin we save 17 trees, 7000 gallons of clean water, 380 gallons of oil, and enough energy to heat a house for six months.

...people in the United States throw away the equivalent of more than thirty million trees in newsprint each year? It takes 75,000 trees to print a Sunday edition of a large city newspaper.

...tin cans are actually 99% steel, with a thin layer of tin added to prevent rusting? It takes four times as much energy to produce a new can as it does to recycle one. Every year, recycling steel saves enough energy to supply three and a half million people with almost 10 year's worth of electricity.

...recycling aluminum cans saves over 95 percent of the energy needed to produce a new can? Last year six out of ten aluminum cans were recycled.

Be An
Earth Smart
Detective:

♦ Can you find in the story all the earth-friendly things Joe and his family did for the party? Hint: there are at least 10 things to find.

♦ Now find the non-earth-friendly things David did at his party. Hint: there are at least 4 things to find.

♦ Turn page upside down to find out the answers.

Answers

Earth friendly things Joe and his family did: had party at home to show how to reduce garbage; built a robot and decorated the treehouse with recyclable materials; told guests not to bring anything that had to be put in the garbage; asked friends to bring bag of recyclables for secret project; used real dishes, glasses and napkins instead of disposables; decorated with reusable ribbons from Grandma's box and flowers from the garden; bought drinks in large glass bottles instead of small boxes; gave ceramic mugs for party favors; put out recycle bins; played games with household objects.

Non-earth-friendly things David did: decorated with paper, helium baloons and styrofoam balls that were thrown out after the party; used paper plates and plastic forks; gave plastic party favors that broke right away; threw everything into the garbage.

29

Test Your Recycling Knowledge

1. When the boys were crushing bags into the garbage can, David's little sister told him that her teacher said we should recycle paper, so we don't have to:
   A) carry so much garbage around.
   B) cut down so many trees and use our land for garbage dumps.
   C) make the street messy with paper.

2. When Justin and Joe were talking on the way home from the party about all the garbage they made, Joe remembered his teacher, Mr. Martin, saying we have to recycle all the time or the earth won't get better. Mr. Martin said that if we cut down all the trees:
   A) we won't even have air to breathe.
   B) we won't be able to have parties.
   C) we won't have birds flying around our neighborhood.

3. When Joe and his mom went shopping for the party they bought two glass bottles of chocolate milk instead of juice boxes, because glass is easier to recycle. Why did they buy ceramic mugs for party favors?

4. Why did Justin bring Joe's present wrapped in the Sunday comics and tied up with ropes of licorice?

5. At the end of the party, Joe's cousin Dan said that if everyone in their school had a wasteful party like David's they would fill the school cafeteria to the ceiling with garbage! But if everyone had an earth-friendly party like Joe's, they would only have a few cans of garbage. What did Joe do at his party that made it better for the environment than David's?

6. Joe made a wish at the end of the party that everyone would think about the earth before they planned parties. At your next party, what are some earth-friendly things you can do that Joe didn't think of?

7. What can you and your family do to celebrate holidays in different ways that would be better for the environment?

Historical Stories for Young Children

These books tell the stories of young women in history who grew up to make significant changes in our society. These picture-story books are fun and riveting for preschoolers and simple enough for an eight year old to read alone.

Elizabeth Blackwell–the story of the first woman doctor.

Juliette Gordon Low–the story of the founder of the Girl Scouts.

Harriet Tubman–the story of the famous conductor on the Underground Railroad.

A Horse's Tale History is told through the eyes of ten children from diverse cultural backgrounds with the help of a wooden horse who gets passed from child to child over 100 years.

The Dealing With Feelings Series:
by Elizabeth Crary

In a choose-your-own-ending format, these books encourage children to find creative ways to express their emotions before the boil-over point.
$5.95 each, 32 pages, illus.

I'm Mad
Katie is furious that rain has cancelled a picnic with her dad.

I'm Frustrated
Alex wants to be able to roller-skate perfectly the first time he tries it, but gets very frustrated when he falls down.

I'm Proud
Mandy rushes to tell her family she's learned to tie her shoes, only to find that everyone is too busy to notice.

Kids to the Rescue!
First Aid Techniques for Kids
by Maribeth and Darwin Boelts
$7.95 paperback, ages 4-12, 72 pgs, illus.

Kids become heroes when they learn first aid! Using an interactive "what would you do if?" format and step-by-step illustrations, this book prompts kids to think wisely in an emergency. The paramedic/teacher writers cover the most common accidents kids encounter. Makes a great teaching tool and a valuable reference.

The Decision is Yours Series:

These books help school-age children think about real-life situations, such as being bullied, finding someone's wallet, or getting a bad report card. The readers make choices for the characters and then see the consequences. Great fun in a no-risk setting!
Ages 7-11, 64 pages, $4.95 each, illus.

Finders, Keepers
by Elizabeth Crary
Decide what Tyrone and Jerry will do with a wallet they find on a hot, summer day.

Bully on the Bus
By Carl W. Bosch
Help Jack deal with the fifth-grade bully at his school.

Making the Grade
by Carl W. Bosch
Help Jenny decide what to do about a bad report card.

First Day Blues
by Peggy King Anderson
Join Megan on her first day at a new school.

Order Form

Name_____

Address_____

City_____St_____Zip_____

Send payment to:
Parenting Press, Inc., Dept. #206,
P.O. Box 75267, Seattle, WA 98125

Or phone for a free catalog:
1-800-992-6657 (9-5 PST)

Shipping	
Book total	Add
$0-$20	$3.95
$20-$50	$4.95
$50-$100	$5.95

Book Total $_____
Shipping   _____
Tax (8.2% for WA) _____
Total $_____
Prices subject to change

Please send me:
__ Elizabeth Blackwell, 5.95
__ Harriet Tubman, 5.95
__ Juliette Gordon Low, 5.95
__ A Horse's Tale, 7.95
__ Kids to the Rescue!, 7.95
__ **Dealing with Feelings Series, $17.85**
__ I'm Mad, 5.95
__ I'm Frustrated, 5.95
__ I'm Proud, 5.95
__ **Decision is Yours Series, $19.80**
__ Bully on the Bus, 4.95
__ Finders, Keepers, 4.95
__ Making the Grade, 4.95
__ First Day Blues, 4.95